CHILDREN'S THRIFT CLASSICS

Black Beauty

(ABRIDGED)

ANNA SEWELL

Illustrated by Thea Kliros

DOVER PUBLICATIONS, INC.
New York

DOVER CHILDREN'S THRIFT CLASSICS
EDITOR: PHILIP SMITH

Published in Canada by General Publishing Company, Ltd., 30 Lesmill Road, Don Mills, Toronto, Ontario.

Published in the United Kingdom by Constable and Company, Ltd., 3 The Lanchesters, 162–164 Fulham Palace Road, London W6 9ER.

This Dover edition, first published in 1993, is a new abridgment of *Black Beauty* (first publication: Jarrold & Sons, London, 1877). The illustrations and introductory Note have been specially prepared for this edition.

Manufactured in the United States of America
Dover Publications, Inc., 31 East 2nd Street, Mineola, N.Y. 11501

Library of Congress Cataloging-in-Publication Data

Black Beauty / Anna Sewell ; illustrated by Thea Kliros. — Abridged.
      p.   cm. — (Dover children's thrift classics)
"This Dover edition, first published in 1993, is a new abridgment of Black Beauty (first publication: Jarrold & Sons, London, 1877). The illustrations and introductory note have been specially prepared for this edition."
    Summary: A horse in nineteenth-century England recounts his experiences with both good and bad masters.
    ISBN 0-486-27570-1
    1. Horses—Juvenile fiction. [1. Horses—Fiction.] I. Kliros, Thea, ill. II. Sewell, Anna, 1820–1878. Black Beauty. III. Series.
PZ10.3.B5624   1993
[Fic]—dc20   93–244
                                                      CIP
                                                      AC

Note

Written by a gentle, bedridden Quakeress, *Black Beauty* (1877) was its author's first and only book, appearing just months before Anna Sewell's death at age fifty-eight. Inspired by a lifelong love of horses and of nature, and guided by the self-improving doctrines of her religion, Sewell crafted a novel that combines a sympathetic understanding of the joys and sufferings of domesticated animals with tractlike, socially conscious pleas for their improved care.

Although the book's initial reception was mild, within a year of publication it had become a phenomenal success, playing a role in countless reform movements and educational programs worldwide. The present abridgment preserves the work's essential narrative and language while shortening the text and omitting some episodes written primarily to effect improvements in the treatment of animals during the author's day.

Contents

List of Illustrations

Part One

THE FIRST PLACE that I can well remember was a large pleasant meadow with a pond of clear water in it. Some shady trees leaned over it, and rushes and water-lilies grew at the deep end. Over the hedge on one side we looked into a plowed field, and on the other we looked over a gate at our master's house, which stood by the roadside; at the top of the meadow was a plantation of fir trees, and at the bottom a running brook overhung by a steep bank.

While I was young I lived upon my mother's milk, as I could not eat grass. In the daytime I ran by her side, and at night I lay down close by her. When I was hot, we used to stand by the pond in the shade of the trees, and when it was cold, we had a nice warm shed near the plantation.

There were six young colts in the meadow besides me; they were older than I was. I used to run with them, and had great fun; we used to gallop all together round and round the field, as hard as we could go. Sometimes we had rather rough play, for they would frequently bite and kick as well as gallop.

One day, when there was a good deal of kicking, my mother whinnied to me to come to her, and then she said: "I wish you to pay attention to what I am going to say to you. The colts who live here are very good colts, but they are cart-horse colts, and, of course, they have not learned manners. You have been well bred and well born; your father has a great name in these parts, and your grandfather won the cup two years at the Newmarket races; your grandmother had the sweetest temper of any horse I ever knew, and I think you have never seen me kick or bite. I hope you will grow up gentle and good, and never learn bad ways; do your work with a good will, lift your feet up well when you trot, and never bite or kick even in play."

I have never forgotten my mother's advice; I knew she was a wise old horse, and our master thought a great deal of her. Her name was Duchess.

Our master was a good, kind man. He gave us good food, good lodging, and kind words; he spoke as kindly to us as he did to his little children. We were all fond of him, and my mother loved him very much. When she saw him at the gate, she would neigh with joy, and trot up to him. All the horses would come to him, but I think we were his favorites. My mother always took him to the town on a market day in a light gig.

Before I was two years old, a circumstance happened which I have never forgotten. It was early in the spring; I and the other colts were feeding at the lower part of the field when we heard, quite in the distance, what sounded like the cry of dogs. The oldest of the colts raised his head, pricked his ears, and said, "There are the hounds!" and immediately cantered off followed by the rest of us to the upper part of the field, where we could look over the hedge and see several fields beyond. My mother and an old riding horse of our master's were also standing near, and seemed to know all about it.

"They have found a hare," said my mother, "and if they come this way we shall see the hunt."

And soon the dogs were all tearing down the field of young wheat next to ours. I never heard such a noise as they made. They did not bark, nor howl, nor whine, but kept on a "yo!

yo, o, o! yo! yo, o, o!" at the top of their voices. After them came a number of men on horseback, all galloping as fast as they could. They were soon away into the fields lower down; here it seemed as if they had come to a stand; the dogs left off barking, and ran about every way with their noses to the ground.

"They have lost the scent," said the old horse, "perhaps the hare will get off."

"What hare?" I said.

"Oh! I don't know *what* hare; any hare they can find will do for the dogs and men to run after"; and before long the dogs began their "yo! yo, o, o!" again, and back they came all together at full speed.

"Now we shall see the hare," said my mother; and just then a hare wild with fright rushed by. On came the dogs, they burst over the bank, leapt the stream, and came dashing across the field, followed by the huntsmen. The hare tried to get through the fence; it was too thick, and she turned sharp round to make for the road, but it was too late; the dogs were upon her with their wild cries; we heard one shriek, and that was the end of her.

As for me, I was so astonished that I did not at first see what was going on by the brook; but when I did look, there was a sad sight; two fine horses were down, one was struggling in the stream, and the other was groaning on the grass. One of the riders was getting out of the water covered with mud, the other lay quite still.

We stood and looked on. Many of the riders had gone to the young man; but my master was the first to raise him. His head fell back and his arms hung down, and everyone looked very serious. There was no noise now; even the dogs were quiet, and seemed to know that something was wrong. They carried him to our master's house. I heard afterwards that it was young George Gordon, the squire's only son, a fine, tall young man, and the pride of his family.

When Mr. Bond, the farrier, came to look at the black horse that lay groaning on the grass, he felt him all over, and shook his head; one of his legs was broken. Then someone ran to our master's house and came back with a gun; presently there was a loud bang and a dreadful shriek, and then all was still; the black horse moved no more.

My mother seemed much troubled; she said she had known that horse for years, and that his name was "Rob Roy"; he was a good bold horse, and there was no vice in him. She never would go to that part of the field afterwards.

Not many days after, we heard the church bell tolling for a long time; and looking over the gate we saw a long strange black coach that was covered with black cloth and was drawn by black horses; after that came another and another and another, and all were black, while the bell kept tolling, tolling. They were carrying young Gordon to the church-yard to bury him. He would never ride again. What they did with Rob Roy I never knew; but 'twas all for one little hare.

.   .   .   .

I was now beginning to grow handsome; my coat had grown fine and soft, and was bright black. I had one white foot, and a pretty white star on my forehead. I was thought very hand-some.

When I was four years old, Squire Gordon came to look at me. He examined my eyes, my mouth, and my legs; and then I had to walk and trot and gallop before him. My master said he would break me in himself, and he lost no time about it, for the next day he began.

Everyone may not know what breaking in is, therefore I will describe it. It means to teach a horse to wear a saddle and bridle and to carry on his back a man, woman, or child.

I was now beginning to grow handsome.

Besides this, he has to learn to have a cart or a chaise fixed behind him, so that he cannot walk or trot without dragging it after him. He must never start at what he sees, nor speak to other horses, nor bite, nor kick, nor have any will of his own; but always do his master's will, even though he may be very tired or hungry; but the worst of all is, when his harness is once on, he may neither jump for joy nor lie down for weariness.

I had of course long been used to be led about in the field and lanes quietly, but now I was to have a bit and a bridle; my master gave me some oats as usual, and, after a good deal of coaxing, he got the bit into my mouth, and the bridle fixed, but it was a nasty thing! Those who have never had a bit in their mouths, cannot think how bad it feels; a great piece of cold hard steel as thick as a man's finger to be pushed into one's mouth, between one's teeth and over one's tongue, with the ends coming out at the corner of your mouth, and held fast there by straps over your head, under your throat, round your nose, and under your chin; so that in no way in the world can you get rid of the nasty hard thing; it is very bad! yes, very bad! at least I thought so; but I knew my mother always wore one when she went out, and all horses did when they were grown up; and so, what with the nice oats, and what with my master's pats, kind words, and gentle ways, I got to wear my bit and bridle.

Next came the saddle, but that was not half so bad; my master put it on my back very gently, then made the girths fast under my body, patting and talking to me all the time; then I had a few oats, then a little leading about, and this he did every day till I began to look for the oats and the saddle. At length, one morning my master got on my back and rode me round the meadow on the soft grass. It certainly did feel queer; but I must say I felt rather proud to carry my master, and as he continued to ride me a little every day, I soon became accustomed to it.

The next unpleasant business was putting on the iron shoes. My master went with me to the smith's forge, to see that I was not hurt or got any fright. The blacksmith took my feet in his hands one after the other, and cut away some of the hoof. It did not pain me, so I stood still on three legs till he had done them all. Then he took a piece of iron the shape of my foot, and clapped it on, and drove some nails through the shoe quite into my hoof, so that the shoe was firmly on. My feet felt very stiff and heavy, but in time I got used to it.

And now having got so far, my master went on to break me to harness; there were more new things to wear. First, a stiff heavy collar just on my neck and a bridle with great side-pieces against my eyes called blinkers, for I could not see on either side, but only straight in front of me; next there was a small saddle with a nasty stiff strap that went right under my tail; that was the crupper.

I must not forget to mention one part of my training, which I have always considered a very great advantage. My master sent me for a fortnight to a neighboring farmer's, who had a meadow which was skirted on one side by the railway. Here were some sheep and cows, and I was turned in among them.

I shall never forget the first train that ran by. I was feeding quietly when I heard a strange sound at a distance, and before I knew whence it came—with a rush and a clatter, and a puffing out of smoke—a long black train flew by, and was gone almost before I could draw my breath. I turned, and galloped to the further side of the meadow as fast as I could go, and there I stood snorting with astonishment and fear. In the course of the day many other trains went by.

For the first few days I could not feed in peace; but as I found that this terrible creature never came into the field, or did me any harm, I began to disregard it, and very soon I cared as little about the passing of a train as the cows and sheep did.

My master often drove me in double harness with my mother, because she was steady, and could teach me how to go better than a strange horse. She told me the better I behaved, the better I should be treated, and that it was wisest always to do my best to please my master. "But," said she, "there are a great many kinds of men; I hope you will fall into good hands; but a horse never knows who may buy him, or who may drive him; it is all a chance for us, but still I say, do your best, wherever it is, and keep up your good name."

Early in May there came a man from Squire Gordon's, who took me away to the Hall. My master said, "Good-bye, be a good horse, and always do your best." I could not say "good-bye," so I put my nose into his hand; he patted me kindly, and I left my first home.

Squire Gordon's Park skirted the village of Birtwick. It was entered by a large iron gate, and a smooth road between clumps of large old trees; then another gate which brought you to the house and the gardens. The stable into which I was taken was very roomy, with four good stalls.

The first stall was a large square one, shut in behind with a wooden gate. Into this fine box the groom put me; it was clean, sweet, and airy. He gave me some very nice oats, he patted me, spoke kindly, and then went away.

When I had eaten my corn I looked round. In the stall next to mine stood a little fat grey pony, with a thick mane and tail, a very pretty head, and a pert little nose.

I put my head up to the iron rails at the top of my box, and said, "How do you do? What is your name?"

He turned round as far as his halter would allow, held up his head, and said, "My name is Merrylegs. I carry the young ladies on my back, and sometimes I take our mistress out in the low chair. Are you going to live next door to me in the box?"

I said, "Yes."

"Well, then," he said, "I hope you are good-tempered; I do not like any one next door who bites."

Just then a horse's head looked over from the stall beyond; the ears were laid back, and the eye looked rather ill-tempered. This was a tall chestnut mare, with a long handsome neck; she looked across to me and said: "So it is you who have turned me out of my box; it is a very strange thing for a colt like you, to come and turn a lady out of her own home."

"I beg your pardon," I said, "I have turned no one out; the man who brought me put me here, and I had nothing to do with it; I never had words yet with horse or mare, and it is my wish to live at peace."

"Well," she said, "we shall see; of course I do not want to have words with a young thing like you." I said no more.

In the afternoon when she went out, Merrylegs told me all about it. "The thing is this," said Merrylegs, "Ginger has a bad habit of biting and snapping; that is why they call her Ginger. Miss Flora and Miss Jessie, who are very fond of me, used to bring me nice things to eat, but after Ginger stood in that box they dare not come, and I missed them very much. I hope they will now come again, if you do not bite or snap."

I told him I never bit anything but grass, hay, and corn, and could not think what pleasure Ginger found in it.

"Well, I don't think she does find pleasure," says Merrylegs; "it is just a bad habit; she says no one was ever kind to her, and why should she not bite? I am sure, if all she says be true, she must have been very ill-used before she came here. John does all he can to please her, so I think she might be good-tempered here. I can tell you there is not a better place for a horse all round the country than this."

. . . .

The name of the coachman was John Manly; he had a wife and one little child, and they lived in the coachman's cottage, very near the stables.

The next morning he took me into the yard and gave me a good grooming, and just as I was going into my box, with my coat soft and bright, the Squire came in to look at me, and seemed pleased. "John," he said, "I meant to have tried the new horse this morning, but I have other business. You may as well take him around after breakfast."

"I will, sir," said John. After breakfast he came and fitted me with a bridle. He was very particular in letting out and taking in the straps, to fit my head comfortably. He rode me first slowly, then a trot, then a canter, and when we were on the common he gave me a light touch with his whip, and we had a splendid gallop.

As we came back through the Park we met the Squire and Mrs. Gordon walking; they stopped, and John jumped off.

"Well, John, how does he go?"

"First-rate, sir," answered John, "he is as fleet as a deer, and has a fine spirit too; but the lightest touch of the rein will guide him."

"That's well," said the Squire, "I will try him myself tomorrow."

The next day I was brought up for my master. I found he was a very good rider, and thoughtful for his horse too. When he came home the lady was at the hall door as he rode up.

"Well, my dear," she said, "how do you like him?"

"He is exactly what John said," he replied; "a pleasanter creature I never wished to mount. What shall we call him?"

She said, "He is really quite a beauty—what do you say to calling him Black Beauty?"

"Black Beauty—why, yes, I think that is a very good name. If you like it shall be his name," and so it was.

When John went into the stable, he told James that master and mistress had chosen a good sensible English name for me, that meant something, not like Marengo, or Pegasus, or Abdallah. They both laughed, and James said, "If it was not for bringing back the past, I should have named him Rob Roy, for I never saw two horses more alike."

"That's no wonder," said John, "didn't you know that Farmer Grey's old Duchess was the mother of them both?"

I had never heard of that before, and so poor Rob Roy who was killed at that hunt was my brother! I did not wonder that my mother was so troubled.

John seemed very proud of me: he used to make my mane and tail almost as smooth as a lady's hair, and he would talk to me a great deal. I grew very fond of him, he was so gentle and kind. James Howard, the stable boy, was just as gentle and pleasant in his way, so I thought myself well off.

A few days after this I had to go out with Ginger in the carriage. I wondered how we should get on together; but except laying her ears back when I was led up to her, she behaved very well. She did her work honestly, and did her full share, and I never wish to have a better partner in double harness. After we had been out two or three times together we grew quite friendly and sociable, which made me feel very much at home.

As for Merrylegs, he and I soon became good friends; he was such a cheerful, plucky, good-tempered little fellow, that he was a favourite with everyone, and especially with Miss Jessie and Flora, who used to ride him about in the orchard, and have fine games with him and their little dog Frisky.

.   .   .   .

Mr. Blomefield, the Vicar, had a large family of boys and girls; sometimes they used to come and play with Miss Jessie and Flora. When they came, there was plenty of work for Merrylegs, for nothing pleased them so much as getting on him by turns and riding him all about the orchard and the home paddock.

One afternoon he had been out with them a long time, and when James brought him in and put on his halter, he said: "There, you rogue, mind how you behave yourself, or we shall get into trouble."

"What have you been doing, Merrylegs?" I asked.

"Oh!" said he, "I have only been giving those young people a lesson, they did not know when they had had enough, nor when I had had enough, so I just pitched them off backwards, that was the only thing they could understand."

"What?" said I, "you threw the children off? I thought you did know better than that! Did you throw Miss Jessie or Miss Flora?"

He looked very much offended, and said: "Of course not. I would not do such a thing for the best oats that ever came into the stable; why, I am as careful of our young ladies as the master could be, and as for the little ones, it is I who teach them to ride. I am the best friend and the best riding master those children have. It is not them, it is the boys; boys," said he, shaking his mane, "are quite different; they must be broken in, as we were broken in when we were colts, and just be taught what's what. The other children had ridden me about for nearly two hours, and then the boys thought it was their turn, and I was quite agreeable. They rode me by turns, and I galloped them about up and down the fields and all about the orchard for a good hour. They had each cut a great hazel stick for a riding whip, and laid it on a little too hard; but I took it in good part, till at last I thought we had had enough, so I stopped two or three times by way of a hint. Boys, you see, think a horse or pony is like a steam engine and can go on as long and as fast as they please; they never think that a pony can get tired, or have any feelings; so as the one who was whipping me could not understand, I just rose up on my hind legs and let him slip off behind—that was all; he mounted me again, and I did the same. Then the other boy got up, and as soon as he began to use his stick I laid him on the

grass, and so on, till they were able to understand, that was all. I like them very well; but
you see I had to give them a lesson."

"If I had been you," said Ginger, "I would
have given those boys a good kick, and that
would have given them a lesson."

"No doubt you would," said Merrylegs, "but
then I am not quite such a fool (begging your
pardon) as to anger our master or make
James ashamed of me; besides, those children
are under my charge when they are riding; I
tell you they are entrusted to me. Do you
think I am such an ungrateful brute as to forget all the kind treatment I have had here for
five years, and all the trust they place in me,
and turn vicious because a couple of ignorant
boys used me badly? No! no! I wouldn't vex
our people for anything; I love them, I do."

One day late in the autumn, my master had
a long journey to go on business. I was put
into the dog-cart, and John went with his master. There had been a great deal of rain, and
now the wind was very high. We went along
merrily till we came to the toll-bar and the
low wooden bridge. The river banks were
rather high, and the bridge, instead of rising,
went across just level, so that if the river was

full, the water would be nearly up to the planks. The man at the gate said the river was rising fast, and he feared it would be a bad night.

When we got to the town, I had a good wait, but as the master's business engaged him a long time, we did not start for home till rather late in the afternoon. The wind was then much higher, and I heard the master say to John, he had never been out in such a storm.

"I wish we were well out of this wood," said my master.

"Yes, sir," said John, "it would be rather awkward if one of these branches came down upon us."

The words were scarcely out of his mouth, when crashing down among the other trees came an oak, right across the road before us. I will never say I was not frightened, for I was. I stopped still, and I believe I trembled; of course, I did not turn round or run away.

"That was a very near touch," said my master. "What's to be done now?"

"Well, sir, we can't drive over that tree nor yet get round it; there will be nothing for it but to go back to the four cross-ways, and that will be a good six miles before we get round to the bridge again; it will make us late, but the horse is fresh."

So back we went, and round by the cross roads; but by the time we got to the bridge it was very nearly dark, we could just see that the water was over the middle of it; but as that happened sometimes when the floods were out, master did not stop. The moment my feet touched the first part of the bridge, I felt sure there was something wrong. I dare not go forward, and I made a dead stop. "Go on, Beauty," said my master, and he gave me a touch with the whip, but I dare not stir; he gave me a sharp cut, I jumped, but I dare not go forward.

"There's something wrong, sir," said John, and he sprang out of the dog-cart and came to my head and looked all about. He tried to lead me forward. "Come on, Beauty, what's the matter?"

Just then the man at the toll-gate on the other side ran out of the house, tossing a torch about like one mad.

"Hoy, hoy, hoy, halloo, stop!" he cried.

"What's the matter?" shouted my master.

"The bridge is broken in the middle and part of it is carried away; if you come on you'll be into the river."

"Thank God!" said my master. "You Beauty!" said John and took the bridle and gently turned me round to the right-hand road by the

"Hoy, hoy, hoy, halloo, stop!" he cried.

river side. I trotted quietly along, the wheels hardly making a sound on the soft road.

At last we came to the Park gates, and found the gardener looking out for us. He said that mistress had been in a dreadful way ever since dark, fearing some accident had happened. We saw a light at the hall door and at the upper windows, and as we came up mistress ran out, saying, "Oh! I have been so anxious, fancying all sorts of things. Have you had no accident?"

"No, my dear; but if your Black Beauty had not been wiser than we were, we should all have been carried down the river." I heard no more, as they went into the house, and John took me to the stable. Oh! what a good supper he gave me that night, a good bran mash and some crushed beans with my oats, and such a thick bed of straw, and I was glad of it, for I was tired.

.   .   .   .

After this, it was decided by my master and mistress to pay a visit to some friends who lived about forty-six miles from our home, and James was to drive them. The first day we travelled thirty-two miles.

We stopped once or twice on the road, and just as the sun was going down we reached the town where we were to spend the night. We stopped at the principal hotel, which was in the Market Place. Two ostlers came to take us out. The head ostler, a pleasant, active little man, led me to a long stable, with six or eight stalls in it, and two or three horses. The other man brought Ginger; James stood by while we were rubbed down and cleaned.

I never was cleaned so lightly and quickly as by that little old man. When he had done, James and the old man left the stable together.

Later on in the evening, a traveller's horse was brought in by the second ostler, and whilst he was cleaning him, a young man with a pipe in his mouth lounged into the stable to gossip.

"I say, Towler," said the ostler, "just run up the ladder into the loft and put some hay down into this horse's rack, will you? only lay down your pipe."

"All right," said the other, and went up through the trap door; and I heard him step across the floor overhead and put down the hay. James came in to look at us the last thing, and then the door was locked.

I cannot say how long I had slept, nor what time in the night it was, but I woke up very uncomfortable. The air seemed all thick and choking: the stable was very full of smoke, and I hardly knew how to breathe. The other horses were all awake; some were pulling at their halters, others were stamping.

At last I heard steps outside, and the ostler who had put up the traveller's horse burst into the stable with a lantern, and began to untie the horses, and try to lead them out. The first horse would not go with him; he tried the second and third, they too would not stir. He tried us all by turns and then left the stable.

No doubt we were very foolish, but danger seemed to be all round, and there was nobody we knew to trust in, and all was strange and uncertain. Then I heard a cry of "Fire" outside, and the old ostler quietly and quickly came in; he got one horse out, and went to another. The next thing I heard was James's voice: "Come, Beauty, on with your bridle, my boy, we'll soon be out of this smother." He took the scarf off his neck, and tied it lightly over my eyes, and patting and coaxing he led me out of the stable.

A tall broad man stepped forward and took me, and James darted back into the stable. I kept my eye fixed on the stable door, where the smoke poured out thicker than ever, and I could see flashes of red light; presently I heard above all the stir and din a loud clear voice, which I knew was master's: "James Howard! James Howard! are you there?" There was no answer, but the next moment I saw James coming through the smoke leading Ginger with him; she was coughing violently, and he was not able to speak.

"My brave lad!" said master, "when you have got your breath, James, we'll get out of this place as quickly as we can."

We got out as fast as we could into the broad quiet Market Place. Master led the way to a large hotel on the other side, and as soon as the ostler came, he said, "James, I must now hasten to your mistress; I trust the horses entirely to you, order whatever you think is needed."

The next morning the master came to see how we were and to speak to James. I could see that James looked very happy, and I thought the master was proud of him.

The rest of our journey was very easy, and a little after sunset we reached the house of my master's friend. We stopped two or three days at this place and then returned home. All went well on the journey; we were glad to be in our own stable again, and John was equally glad to see us.

. . . .

I saw James coming through the smoke
leading Ginger.

Soon afterward, James left us, having secured a position as a groom for our master's brother-in-law. In his place came Joe Green, a local lad of but fourteen and a half years. One night, a few days after James had left, I was lying down in my straw fast asleep, when I was suddenly awoke by the stable bell ringing very loud. I heard the door of John's house open, and his feet running up to the Hall. He was back again in no time; he unlocked the stable door, and came in, calling out, "Wake up, Beauty, you must go well now, if ever you did," and almost before I could think, he had got the saddle on my back and the bridle on my head; he just ran round for his coat, and then took me at a quick trot up to the Hall door. The Squire stood there with a lamp in his hand.

"Now, John," he said, "ride for your life, that is, for your mistress's life; there is not a moment to lose; give this note to Doctor White; give your horse a rest at the Inn, and be back as soon as you can."

John said, "Yes, sir," and was on my back in a minute. The gardener who lived at the lodge had heard the bell ring, and was ready with the gate open, and away we went through the Park and through the village, and down the hill.

There was before us a long piece of level road by the river side; John said to me, "Now Beauty, do your best," and so I did; I don't believe that my old grandfather who won the race at Newmarket could have gone faster. The church clock struck three as we drew up at Doctor White's door. John rang the bell twice, and then knocked at the door like thunder. A window was thrown up, and Doctor White put his head out and said, "What do you want?"

"Mrs. Gordon is very ill, sir; master wants you to go at once, he thinks she will die if you cannot get there—here is a note."

"Wait," he said, "I will come." He shut the window, and was soon at the door. "The worst of it is," he said, "that my horse has been out all day and is quite done up; my son has just been sent for, and he has taken the other. What is to be done? Can I have your horse?"

"He has come at a gallop nearly all the way, sir, and I was to give him a rest here; but I think my master would not be against it if you think fit, sir."

"All right," he said, "I will soon be ready."

I will not tell about our way back; the Doctor was a heavier man than John, and not so good a rider; however, I did my very best, and soon we were in the Park. My master was at the Hall door, for he had heard us coming. He spoke not a word; the Doctor went into the house with him, and Joe led me to the stable. I had not a dry hair on my body, the water ran down my legs, and I steamed all over—Joe used to say, like a pot on the fire. Poor Joe! he did the very best he knew. He rubbed my legs and my chest, but he did not put my warm cloth on me; he thought I was so hot I should not like it. Then he gave me a pail full of water and I drank it all; then he gave me some hay and some corn, and went away. Soon I began to shake and tremble, and turned deadly cold. Oh! how I wished for my warm thick cloth as I stood and trembled. After a long while I heard John at the door; I gave a low moan, for I was now very ill; a strong inflammation had attacked my lungs, and I could not draw my breath without pain. John nursed me night and day; my master, too, often came to see me.

"My poor Beauty," he said one day, "my good horse, you saved your mistress' life, Beauty!" I was very glad to hear that, for it seems the Doctor had said if we had been a little longer it would have been too late. John told my master he never saw a horse go so fast in his life, it seemed as if the horse knew what was the matter. Of course I did, though

John thought not; at least I knew as much as this, that John and I must go at the top of our speed, and that it was for the sake of the mistress.

I do not know how long I was ill. The horse doctor came every day. One day he bled me; John held a pail for the blood; I felt very faint after it, and thought I should die, and I believe they all thought so too, but at length I regained my health.

.   .   .   .

I had now lived in this happy place three years, but sad changes were about to come over us. Our mistress was ill. The Doctor was often at the house, and the master looked grave and anxious. Then we heard that she must go to a warm country for two or three years. Everybody was sorry; but the master began directly to make arrangements for breaking up his establishment.

The first of the party who went were Miss Jessie and Flora with their governess. They hugged poor Merrylegs like an old friend, and so indeed he was. Then we heard what had been arranged for us. Master had sold Ginger and me to his old friend, the Earl of W——, for he thought we should have a good place there. Merrylegs he had given to the Vicar, on the condition that he should never be sold, and when he was past work that he should be shot and buried.

The evening before they left, the master came into the stable to give some directions and to give his horses the last pat. "Have you decided what to do, John?" he said.

"No, sir. I have made up my mind that if I could get a situation with some first-rate colt-breaker and horse-trainer, that it would be the right thing for me. I always get on well with horses, and if I could help some of them to a fair start, I should feel as if I was doing some good."

"I don't know a man anywhere," said master, "that I should think so suitable for it as yourself. If in any way I can help you, write to me; I shall speak to my agent in London, and leave your character with him." Master gave John his hand, but he did not speak, and they both left the stable.

The last sad day had come; Ginger and I brought the carriage up to the Hall door for the last time. The servants brought out cushions and rugs and master came down the steps carrying the mistress in his arms; he placed her carefully in the carriage, while the house servants stood round crying. "Good-bye, again," he said, "we shall not forget any of you," and he got in—"Drive on, John."

Joe jumped up, and we trotted slowly through the Park, and through the village, where the people were standing at their doors to have a last look and to say, "God bless them."

When we reached the railway station, I think mistress walked from the carriage to the waiting room. As soon as Joe had taken the things out of the carriage, John called him to stand by the horses, while he went on the platform. Poor Joe! he stood close up to our heads to hide his tears. Very soon the train came puffing up into the station; then two or three minutes, and the doors were slammed to; the guard whistled and the train glided away, leaving behind it only clouds of white smoke, and some very heavy hearts.

When it was quite out of sight, John came back: "We shall never see her again," he said—"never." He took the reins, mounted the box, and with Joe drove slowly home; but it was not our home now.

Part Two

THE NEXT MORNING after breakfast Joe put Merrylegs into the mistress's low chaise to take him to the vicarage; he came first and said good-bye to us, and Merrylegs neighed to us from the yard. Then John put the saddle on Ginger and the leading rein on me, and rode us across the country about fifteen miles to Earlshall Park, where the Earl of W—— lived. There was a very fine house and a great deal of stabling; we went into the yard through a stone gateway, and John asked for Mr. York. It was some time before he came. He was a fine-looking, middle-aged man, and his voice said at once that he expected to be obeyed. He was very friendly and polite to John, and after giving us a slight look he called a groom to take us to our boxes, and invited John to take some refreshment.

We were taken to a light, airy stable, and placed in boxes adjoining each other, where we were rubbed down and fed. In about half-an-hour John and Mr. York, who was to be our new coachman, came in to see us.

"Now, Mr. Manly," he said, after carefully looking at us both, "I can see no fault in these horses, but I should like to know if there is anything particular in either of these that you would like to mention."

"Well," said John, "I don't believe there is a better pair of horses in the country, but they are not alike. The black one is the most perfect temper I ever knew; but the chestnut I fancy must have had bad treatment. She came to us snappish and suspicious, but when she found what sort of place ours was, it all went off by degrees; for three years I have never seen the smallest sign of temper, but she is naturally a more irritable constitution than the black horse; and if she were ill-used or unfairly treated, she would not be unlikely to give tit for tat; you know that many high-mettled horses will do so."

"Of course," said York, "but you know it is not easy in stables like these to have all the grooms just what they should be; I do my best, and there I must leave it. I'll remember what you have said about the mare."

They were going out of the stable when John stopped and said, "I had better mention that we have never used the 'bearing rein' with either of them; the black horse never had one on."

"Well," said York, "if they come here they must wear the bearing rein. I prefer a loose rein myself, and his lordship is always very reasonable about horses; but my lady—that's another thing—she will have style; and if her carriage horses are not reined up tight, she wouldn't look at them. I always stand out against the gag-bit, but it must be tight up when my lady rides!"

"I am sorry for it, very sorry," said John, "but I must go now, or I shall lose the train."

The next day Lord W—— came to look at us; he seemed pleased with our appearance. "I have great confidence in these horses," he said, "from the character my friend Mr. Gordon has given me of them. Of course they are not a match in colour, but my idea is that they will do very well for the carriage while we are in the country."

York then told him what John had said about us.

"Well," said he, "you must keep an eye to the mare, and put the bearing rein easy; I dare say they will do very well with a little humouring at first."

In the afternoon we were harnessed and put

in the carriage, and led round to the front of the house. It was all very grand, and three or four times as large as the old house at Birtwick, but not half so pleasant. Two footmen were standing ready, dressed in drab livery, with scarlet breeches and white stockings.

Presently we heard the rustling sound of silk as my lady came down the flight of stone steps. She stepped around to look at us; she was a tall, proud-looking woman, and did not seem pleased about something, but she said nothing, and got into the carriage. This was the first time of wearing a bearing rein, and though it certainly was a nuisance not to be able to get my head down now and then, it did not pull my head higher than I was accustomed to carry it. I felt anxious about Ginger, but she seemed to be quiet and content.

The next day we were again at the door, and the footmen as before; we heard the silk dress rustle, and the lady came down the steps, and in an imperious voice she said, "York, you must put those horses' heads higher; they are not fit to be seen."

York got down and said very respectfully, "I beg your pardon, my lady, but these horses have not been reined up for three years, and my lord said it would be safer to bring them to it by degrees; but if your ladyship pleases, I can take them up a little more."

"Do so," she said.

Day by day, hole by hole our bearing reins were shortened, and instead of looking forward with pleasure to having my harness put on as I used to do, I began to dread it. Ginger too seemed restless, though she said very little.

One day my lady came down later than usual, and the silk rustled more than ever.

"Drive to the Duchess of B——'s," she said, and then after a pause, "Are you never going to get those horses' heads up, York? Raise them at once."

York came to me first. He drew my head back and fixed the rein so tight that it was almost intolerable; then he went to Ginger. She had a good idea of what was coming, and the moment York took the rein in order to shorten it, she took her opportunity and reared up so suddenly that York had his nose roughly hit, and his hat knocked off; the groom was nearly thrown off his legs. At once they both flew to her head, but she was a match for them, and went on plunging, rearing, and kicking in a most desperate manner; at last she kicked right over the carriage pole and fell down, after giving me a severe blow on my near quarter. York promptly sat himself down flat on her head to prevent her struggling, at the same time calling out, "Unbuckle the black horse!" The groom soon set me free from Ginger and the carriage, and led me to my box.

Before long, Ginger was led in by two grooms, a good deal knocked about and bruised. York came with her and gave his orders, and then came to look at me. He felt me all over, and soon found the place above my hock where I had been kicked. It was swelled and painful; he ordered it to be sponged with hot water, and then some lotion was put on.

Ginger was never put into the carriage again but when she was well of her bruises, one of Lord W—'s younger sons, Lord George, said he should like to have her; he was sure she would make a good hunter. As for me, I was obliged still to go in the carriage, and had a fresh partner called Max; he had always been used to the tight rein.

What I suffered with that rein for four long months in my lady's carriage, it would be hard to describe; but I am quite sure that, had it lasted much longer, either my health or my temper would have given way. Before that, I never knew what it was to foam at the mouth,

but now the action of the sharp bit on my
tongue and jaw, and the constrained position
of my head and throat always caused me to
froth at the mouth more or less.

In my old home I always knew that John
and my master were my friends; but here,
although in many ways I was well treated, I
had no friend. York might have known, and
very likely did know, how that rein harassed
me; but I suppose he took it as a matter of
course that could not be helped; at any rate,
nothing was done to relieve me.

. . . .

Early in the spring, Lord W—— and part of
his family went up to London, and took York
with them. I and Ginger and some other
horses were left at home for use, and the head
groom was left in charge.

The Lady Harriet, who remained at the Hall,
was a great invalid, and never went out in the
carriage, and the Lady Anne preferred riding
on horseback with her brother, or cousins.
She was a perfect horsewoman, and as gay
and gentle as she was beautiful. She chose me
for her horse, and named me "Black Auster." I
enjoyed these rides very much in the clear
cold air, sometimes with Ginger, sometimes
with Lizzie, a bright bay mare.

There was a gentleman of the name of Blantyre staying at the Hall; he always rode Lizzie,
and praised her so much that one day Lady
Anne ordered the side-saddle to be put on her,
and the other saddle on me. When we came to
the door, the gentleman seemed very uneasy.
"How is this?" he said, "are you tired of your
good Black Auster?"

"Oh! no, not at all," she replied, "but I am
amiable enough to let you ride him for once,
and I will try your charming Lizzie. You must
confess she is far more like a lady's horse
than my own favourite."

"Do let me advise you not to mount her," he
said, "she is a charming creature, but she is
too nervous for a lady."

"My dear cousin," said Lady Anne, laughing,
"pray do not trouble your good careful head
about me; I have been a horsewoman ever
since I was a baby, and I have followed the
hounds a great many times. I intend to try this
Lizzie, so please help me to mount."

There was no more to be said. Just as we
were moving off, a footman came out with a
slip of paper and message from the Lady
Harriet—"Would they ask this question for
her at Dr. Ashley's, and bring the answer?"

The village was about a mile off, and the
Doctor's house was the last in it. We went

along gaily enough till we came to his gate.
Blantyre alighted at the gate, and was going to
open it for Lady Anne, but she said, "I will
wait for you here, and you can hang Auster's
rein on the gate."

He looked at her doubtfully—"I will not be
five minutes," he said.

"Oh, do not hurry yourself. Lizzie and I shall
not run away from you."

He hung my rein on one of the iron spikes,
and was soon hidden among the trees. Lizzie
was standing quietly by the side of the road a
few paces off with her back to me. My young
mistress was sitting easily with a loose rein,
humming a little song. I listened to my rider's
footsteps until they reached the house, and
heard him knock at the door. There was a
meadow on the opposite side of the road, the
gate of which stood open. Just then some cart
horses and several young colts came trotting
out in a very disorderly manner, while a boy
behind was cracking a great whip. The colts
were wild and frolicsome, and one of them
bolted across the road, and blundered up
against Lizzie's hind legs; she gave a violent
kick, and dashed off into a headlong gallop. It
was so sudden that Lady Anne was nearly
unseated, but she soon recovered herself.
Blantyre came running to the gate; he looked

Giving me a free rein, we dashed after them.

anxiously about, and just caught sight of the flying figure, now far away on the road. In an instant he sprang into the saddle, and giving me a free rein, we dashed after them.

For about a mile and a half the road ran straight, and then bent to the right, after which it divided into two roads. Long before we came to the bend, she was out of sight. A woman was standing at her garden gate, looking eagerly up the road. Blantyre shouted, "Which way?" "To the right," cried the woman, pointing, and away we went up the right-hand road; then for a moment we caught sight of her; another bend and she was hidden again. Several times we caught glimpses, and then lost them. An old road-mender was standing near a heap of stones, his hands raised. As we came near he made a sign to speak. Blantyre drew the rein a little. "To the common, to the common, sir; she has turned off there."

We had hardly turned on the common, when we caught sight again of the green habit flying on before us. My lady's hat was gone, and her long brown hair was streaming behind her. It was clear that the roughness of the ground had very much lessened Lizzie's speed, and there seemed a chance that we might overtake her.

About halfway across the heath there had

been a wide dyke recently cut, and the earth from the cutting was cast up roughly on the other side. With scarcely a pause Lizzie took the leap, stumbled among the rough clods, and fell. Blantyre gave me a steady rein. I gathered myself well together, and with one determined leap cleared both dyke and bank.

Motionless among the heather, with her face to the earth, lay my poor young mistress. Blantyre kneeled down and called her name— there was no sound; gently he turned her face upward, it was ghastly white, and the eyes were closed. He unbuttoned her habit, loosened her collar, felt her hands and wrists, then started up and looked wildly round him for help.

At no great distance there were two men cutting turf, who seeing Lizzie running wild without a rider had left their work to catch her. Blantyre's halloo soon brought them to the spot. The foremost man asked what he could do.

"Can you ride?"

"Well, sir, I bean't much of a horseman, but I'd risk my neck for the Lady Anne; she was uncommon good to my wife in the winter."

"Then mount this horse, my friend, and ride to the Doctor's and ask him to come instantly—then on to the Hall—bid them send me the carriage with Lady Anne's maid and help. I shall stay here."

"All right, sir, I'll do my best, and I pray God the dear young lady may open her eyes soon." He then somehow scrambled into the saddle, and with a "Gee-up" and a clap on my sides with both his legs, he started on his journey. I shook him as little as I could help, but once or twice on the rough ground he called out, "Steady! Woa! Steady!" On the high road we were all right; and at the Doctor's and the Hall he did his errand like a good man and true.

There was a great deal of hurry and excitement after the news became known. I was just turned into my box, and a cloth thrown over me. Ginger was saddled and sent off in great haste for Lord George, and I soon heard the carriage roll out of the yard.

It seemed a long time before Ginger came back and before we were left alone; and then she told me all that she had seen. "I can't tell much," she said; "we went a gallop nearly all the way, and got there just as the Doctor rode up. There was a woman sitting on the ground with the lady's head in her lap. The Doctor poured something into her mouth, but all that I heard was 'she is not dead.' After a while she was taken to the carriage, and we came home together. I heard my master say to a gentleman who stopped him to inquire, that he hoped no bones were broken, but that she had not spoken yet."

Two days after the accident, Blantyre paid me a visit; he patted me and praised me very much, he told Lord George that he was sure the horse knew of Annie's danger as well as he did. I found by their conversation that my young mistress was now out of danger, and would soon be able to ride again. This was good news to me, and I looked forward to a happy life.

.   .   .   .

Reuben Smith was left in charge of the stables when York went to London. No one more thoroughly understood his business than he did, and when he was all right, there could not be a more faithful or valuable man. I believe everybody liked him; certainly the horses did; the only wonder was that he should be in an under situation, and not in the place of a head coachman like York: but he had one great fault, and that was the love of drink.

It was now early in April, and the family was expected home some time in May. The light brougham was to be freshly done up, and as Colonel Blantyre was obliged to return to his regiment, it was arranged that Smith should drive him to the town in it, and ride back; for this purpose, he took the saddle with him, and I was chosen for the journey. At the station the Colonel put some money into Smith's hand and bid him good-bye.

We left the carriage at the maker's, and Smith rode me to the White Lion, and ordered the ostler to feed me well and have me ready for him at four o'clock. A nail in one of my front shoes had started as I came along, but the ostler did not notice it till just about four o'clock. Smith did not come into the yard till five, and then he said he should not leave till six, as he had met with some old friends. The man then told him of the nail, and asked if he should have the shoe looked to.

"No," said Smith, "that will be all right till we get home." He spoke in a very loud offhand way, and I thought it very unlike him, not to see about loose nails in our shoes. He did not come at six, nor seven, nor eight, and it was nearly nine o'clock before he called for me, and then it was in a loud rough voice. He seemed in a very bad temper, and almost before he was out of the town he began to gallop, frequently giving me a sharp cut with his whip, though I was going at full speed. The moon had not yet risen, and it was very dark. The roads were stony, having been recently mended; going over them at this pace my shoe became looser and when we were near the turnpike gate it came off.

Beyond the turnpike was a long piece of road, upon which fresh stones had just been laid; large sharp stones, over which no horse could be driven quickly without risk of danger. Over this road, with one shoe gone, I was forced to gallop at my utmost speed. Of course my shoeless foot suffered dreadfully; the hoof was broken and split down to the very quick, and the inside was terribly cut by the sharpness of the stones.

This could not go on; no horse could keep his footing under such circumstances; the pain was too great. I stumbled, and fell with violence on both my knees. Smith was flung off by my fall, and owing to the speed I was going at, he must have fallen with great force. I soon recovered my feet and limped to the side of the road. The moon had just risen above the hedge, and by its light I could see Smith lying a few yards beyond me. He did not rise, he made one slight effort to do so, and then there was a heavy groan. I uttered no sound, but I stood there and listened. One more heavy groan from Smith; but though he now lay in the full moonlight, I could see no motion. The road was not much frequented, and at this time of the night we might stay for hours before help came to us.

It must have been nearly midnight when I heard at a great distance the sound of a horse's feet. As the sound came nearer and nearer, I was almost sure I could distinguish Ginger's step; a little nearer still, and I could tell she was in the dog-cart. I neighed loudly, and was overjoyed to hear an answering neigh from Ginger, and men's voices. They came slowly over the stones, and stopped at the dark figure that lay upon the ground.

One of the men jumped out, and stooped down over it. "It is Reuben!" he said.

The other man followed and bent over him. "He's dead," he said; "feel how cold his hands are."

They raised him up, but there was no life, and his hair was soaked with blood. They laid him down again, and came and looked at me. They soon saw my cut knees.

"Why, the horse has been down and thrown him! Who would have thought the black horse would have done that? Nobody thought he could fall."

Robert then attempted to lead me forward. I made a step, but almost fell again. "Hallo! he's bad in his foot as well as his knees; look here—his hoof is cut all to pieces, he might well come down, poor fellow! I tell you what, Ned, I'm afraid it hasn't been all right with Reuben! Just think of him riding a horse over these stones without a shoe!"

It was agreed that Robert as the groom should lead me, and that Ned must take the body. Ned started off with his sad load, and Robert came and looked at my foot again; then he led me on very slowly, and I limped and hobbled on as well as I could with great pain.

The next day, after the farrier had examined my wounds, he said he hoped the joint was not injured, and if so, I should not be spoiled for work, but I should never lose the blemish. I believe they did the best to make a good cure, but it was a long and painful one.

.   .   .   .

As soon as my knees were sufficiently healed, I was turned into a small meadow for a month or two; no other creature was there, and though I enjoyed the liberty and the sweet grass, yet I felt very lonely. Ginger and I had become fast friends, and now I missed her company extremely. I often neighed when I heard horses' feet passing in the road, but I seldom got an answer; till one morning the gate opened, and who should come in but dear old Ginger. With a joyful whinny I trotted up to her; we were both glad to meet, but I soon found that it was not for our pleasure that she was brought to be with me. She had been ruined by hard riding, and was now turned off to see what rest would do.

One day we saw the Earl come into the meadow, and York was with him. They examined us carefully. The Earl seemed much annoyed.

"There is three hundred pounds flung away for no earthly use," said he; "but what I care most for is that these horses of my old friend, who thought they would find a good home with me, are ruined. The mare shall have a twelve-month's run, and we shall see what that will do for her; but the black one, he must be sold; 'tis a great pity, but I could not have knees like these in my stables."

"No, my lord, of course not," said York; "but he might get a place where his appearance is not of much consequence, and still be well treated. I know a man in Bath, the master of some livery stables, who often wants a good horse at a low figure; I know he looks well after his horses." After this they left us.

"They'll soon take you away," said Ginger,

"and I shall lose the only friend I have, and most likely we shall never see each other again. 'Tis a hard world!"

About a week after this, Robert came into the field with a halter, which he slipped over my head, and led me away. Through the recommendation of York I was bought by the master of the livery stables. These stables were not so airy and pleasant as those I had been used to; however, I was well fed and well cleaned, and, on the whole, I think our master took as much care of us as he could. He kept a good many horses and carriages of different kinds for hire. Sometimes his own men drove them; at others, the horse and chaise were let to gentlemen or ladies who drove themselves.

Hitherto I had always been driven by people who at least knew how to drive; but in this place I was to get my experience of all the different kinds of bad and ignorant driving to which we horses are subjected.

One morning I was put into the light gig, and taken to a house in Pulteney Street. Two gentlemen came out; the taller of them came round to my head, he looked at the bit and bridle, and just shifted the collar with his hand to see if it fitted comfortably.

"Do you consider this horse wants a curb?" he said to the ostler. "Be so good as to take it off, and put the rein in at the cheek; an easy mouth is a great thing on a long journey, is it not, old fellow?" he said, patting my neck.

I arched my neck and set off at my best pace. I found I had someone behind me who knew how a good horse ought to be driven. It seemed like old times again, and made me feel quite gay.

This gentleman took a great liking to me, and after trying me several times with the saddle he prevailed upon my master to sell me to a friend of his, who wanted a safe pleasant horse for riding. And so it came to pass that in the summer I was sold to Mr. Barry.

My new master was an unmarried man. His doctor advised him to take horse exercise, and for this purpose he bought me. He hired a stable a short distance from his lodgings, and engaged a man named Filcher as groom. My master knew very little about horses, but he treated me well, and I should have had a good and easy place but for circumstances of which he was ignorant.

After a while it seemed to me that my oats

came very short; certainly not more than a quarter of what there should have been. In two or three weeks this began to tell upon my strength and spirits. However, I could not complain, nor make known my wants. So it went on for about two months; and I wondered my master did not see that something was the matter. However, one afternoon he rode out into the country to see a friend of his—a gentleman farmer, who lived on the road to Wells. This gentleman had a very quick eye for horses; and after he had welcomed his friend, he said, casting his eye over me: "It seems to me, Barry, that your horse does not look so well as he did when you first had him. Has he been well?"

"Yes, I believe so," said my master, "but he is not nearly so lively as he was; my groom tells me that horses are always dull and weak in the autumn, and that I must expect it."

"Autumn! fiddlesticks!" said the farmer. "I advise you to look into your stable a little more. I hate to be suspicious, but there are mean scoundrels, wicked enough to rob a dumb beast of his food; you must look into it."

My groom used to come every morning about six o'clock, and with him a little boy, who used to go with his father into the harness room where the corn was kept, and fill a little bag with oats out of the bin and then be off.

Five or six mornings after this, just as the boy had left the stable, the door was pushed open and a policeman walked in, holding the child tight by the arm; another policeman followed, and locked the door on the inside, saying, "Show me the place where your father keeps his rabbits' food."

The boy looked very frightened and began to cry; but there was no escape, and he led the way to the corn-bin. Here the policemen found another empty bag like that which was found full of oats in the boy's basket.

Filcher was cleaning my feet at the time, and though he blustered a good deal, they walked him off to the "lock-up," and the man was sentenced to prison for two months.

In a few days my new groom came. He was a tall, good-looking fellow enough; he always brushed my mane and tail with water, and my hoofs with oil before he brought me to the door, to make me look smart; but as to cleaning my feet, or looking to my shoes, or grooming me thoroughly, he thought no more of that than if I had been a cow. I should say he was the laziest, most conceited fellow I ever came near.

One day my feet were so tender, that trot-

ting over some fresh stones with my master
on my back, I made two such serious stum-
bles, that he stopped at the farrier's and asked
him to see what was the matter with me. The
man took up my feet one by one and examined them; then he said:

"Your horse has got the 'thrush,' and badly
too; his feet are very tender; it is fortunate
that he has not been down. I wonder your
groom has not seen to it before. This is the
sort of thing we find in foul stables, where the
litter is never properly cleared out."

The next day I had my feet thoroughly
cleansed and stuffed with tow, soaked in
some strong lotion; and a very unpleasant
business it was.

With this treatment I soon regained my
spirits, but Mr. Barry was so much disgusted
at being twice deceived by his grooms that he
determined to give up keeping a horse, and to
hire when he wanted one. I was therefore
kept till my feet were quite sound, and was
then sold again.

Part Three

NO DOUBT a horse fair is a very amusing place to those who have nothing to lose; at any rate, there is plenty to see.

Long strings of young horses out of the country, fresh from the marshes; and droves of shaggy little Welsh ponies, no higher than Merrylegs; and hundreds of cart horses of all sorts; and a good many like myself, handsome and high-bred, but fallen into the middle class, through some accident or blemish, unsoundness of wind, or some other complaint. There were some splendid animals quite in their prime, and fit for anything; they were throwing out their legs and showing off their paces in high style. But round in the background there were a number of poor things, sadly broken down with hard work; with their knees knuckling over, and their hind legs swinging out at every step; and there were some very dejected-looking old horses, with the under lip hanging down, and the ears lay-

ing back heavily, as if there was no more pleasure in life, and no more hope; there were
some so thin, you might see all their ribs, and
some with old sores on their backs and hips;
these were sad sights for a horse to look
upon, who knows not but he may come to the
same state.

I was put with two or three other strong,
useful-looking horses, and a good many people came to look at us. The gentlemen always
turned from me when they saw my broken
knees; though the man who had me swore it
was only a slip in the stall.

There was one man, I thought, if he would
buy me, I should be happy. He was not a gentleman, nor yet one of the loud flashy sort that
called themselves so. He was rather a small
man, but well made and quick in all his
motions. I knew in a moment, by the way he
handled me, that he was used to horses; he
spoke gently, and his grey eye had a kindly,
cheery look in it. He offered twenty-three
pounds for me; but that was refused, and he
walked away. I looked after him, but he was
gone, and a very hard-looking, loud-voiced
man came. I was dreadfully afraid he would
have me; but he walked off. One or two more
came who did not mean business. Then the
hard-faced man came back again and offered

twenty-three pounds. A very close bargain was being driven; for my salesman began to think he should not get all he asked, and must come down; but just then the grey-eyed man came back again. I could not help reaching out my head towards him. He stroked my face kindly.

"Well, old chap," he said, "I think we should suit each other. I'll give twenty-four for him."

"Say twenty-five and you shall have him."

"Twenty-four ten," said my friend, in a very decided tone, "and not another sixpence—yes or no?"

"Done," said the salesman, "and you may depend upon it there's a monstrous deal of quality in that horse, and if you want him for cab work, he's a bargain."

The money was paid on the spot, and my new master took my halter, and led me out of the fair to an inn, where he had a saddle and bridle ready. He gave me a good feed of oats and stood by whilst I ate it, talking to himself and talking to me. Half-an-hour after, we were on our way to London, through pleasant lanes and country roads, until we came into the great London thoroughfare, on which we traveled steadily, till in the twilight we reached the great city. The gas lamps were already lighted; there were streets crossing each other for mile upon mile. I thought we should never come to the end of them. At last, in passing through one, we came to a long cab stand, where my rider called out in a cheery voice, "Good night, Governor!"

"Halloo!" cried a voice, "have you got a good one?"

"I think so," replied my owner.

"I wish you luck with him."

"Thank ye, Governor," and he rode on. We soon turned up one of the side streets, and about half-way up that, we turned into a very narrow street, with rather poor-looking houses on one side, and what seemed to be coach-houses and stables on the other.

My owner pulled up at one of the houses and whistled. The door flew open, and a young woman, followed by a little girl and boy, ran out. There was a very lively greeting as my rider dismounted.

"Now, then, Harry, my boy, open the gates, and mother will bring us the lantern."

The next minute they were all standing round me in a small stable yard.

"Is he gentle, father?"

"Yes, Dolly, as gentle as your own kitten; come and pat him." At once the little hand was patting about all over my shoulder without fear. How good it felt!

My owner pulled up at one of the houses
and whistled.

"Let me get him a bran mash while you rub him down," said the mother.

"Do, Polly, it's just what he wants, and I know you've got a beautiful mash ready for me."

.   .   .   .

My new master's name was Jeremiah Barker, but every one called him Jerry. Polly, his wife, was just as good a match as a man could have. She was a plump, trim, tidy little woman, with smooth dark hair, dark eyes, and a merry little mouth. The boy was nearly twelve years old: a tall, frank, good-tempered lad; and little Dorothy (Dolly they called her) was her mother over again, at eight years old. They were all wonderfully fond of each other; I never knew such a happy, merry family before, or since. Jerry had a cab of his own, and two horses, which he drove and attended to himself. His other horse was a tall, white, rather large-boned animal called Captain; he was old now, but when he was young, he must have been splendid; he was a high-bred, fine-mannered, noble old horse. He told me that in his early youth he went to the Crimean War; he belonged to an officer in the cavalry, and used to lead the regiment.

The next morning, when I was well

groomed, Polly and Dolly came into the yard to see me and make friends. Harry had been helping his father since the early morning, and had stated his opinion that I should turn out "a regular brick." Polly brought me a slice of apple, and Dolly a piece of bread. It was a great treat to be petted again, and talked to in a gentle voice, and I let them see as well as I could that I wished to be friendly. Polly thought I was very handsome, and a great deal too good for a cab, if it was not for the broken knees.

"Of course there's no one to tell us whose fault that was," said Jerry, "and as long as I don't know, I shall give him the benefit of the doubt; for a firmer, neater stepper I never rode; we'll call him 'Jack,' after the old one— shall we, Polly?"

"Do," she said, "for I like to keep a good name going."

Captain went out in the cab all the morning. Harry came in after school to feed me and give me water. In the afternoon I was put into the cab. Jerry took as much pains to see if the collar and bridle fitted comfortably as if he had been John Manly over again. There was no bearing rein—no curb—nothing but a plain ring snaffle. What a blessing that was!

After driving through the side street we

came to the large cab stand where Jerry had
said "Good night." On one side of this wide
street were high houses with wonderful shop
fronts, and on the other was an old church
and churchyard, surrounded by iron pali-
sades. Alongside these iron rails a number of
cabs were drawn up, waiting for passengers.
We pulled up in the rank at the back of the
last cab. Two or three men came round and
began to look at me and pass their remarks.

"Very good for a funeral," said one.

"Too smart-looking," said another, shaking
his head in a very wise way; "you'll find out
something wrong one of these fine mornings,
or my name isn't Jones."

"Well," said Jerry pleasantly, "I suppose I
need not find it out till it finds me out; eh?"

Then came up a broad-faced man, dressed
in a great grey coat with great grey capes, and
great white buttons, a grey hat, and a blue
comforter loosely tied round his neck; his hair
was grey too, but he was a jolly-looking fellow, and the other men made way for him. He
looked me all over, as if he had been going
to buy me; and then, straightening himself
up with a grunt, he said, "He's the right sort
for you, Jerry. I don't care what you gave for
him, he'll be worth it." Thus my character was
established on the stand.

This man's name was Grant, but he was called "Grey Grant," or "Governor Grant." He had been the longest on that stand of any of the men, and he took it upon himself to settle matters and stop disputes.

The first week of my life as a cab horse was very trying; I had never been used to London, and the noise, the hurry, the crowds of horses, carts, and carriages that I had to make my way through made me feel anxious and harassed; but I soon found that I could perfectly trust my driver, and then I made myself easy, and got used to it.

Jerry was as good a driver as I had ever known; and what was better, he took as much thought for his horses as he did for himself. He never laid the whip on me, unless it was gently drawing the end of it over my back, when I was to go on; but generally I knew this quite well by the way in which he took up the reins; and I believe his whip was more frequently stuck up by his side than in his hand.

In a short time I and my master understood each other as well as horse and man can do. In the stable, too, he did all that he could for our comfort. The stalls were the old-fashioned style, too much on the slope; but he had two movable bars fixed across the back of our stalls, so that at night, and when we were rest-ing, he just took off our halters and put up the bars, and thus we could turn about and stand whichever way we pleased, which is a great comfort.

Jerry kept us very clean, and gave us as much change of food as he could, and always plenty of it; and not only that, but he always gave us plenty of clean, fresh water, which he allowed to stand by us both night and day, except of course when we came in warm. But the best thing that we had here was our Sundays for rest; we worked so hard in the week that I do not think we could have kept up to it, but for that day; besides, we had then time to enjoy each other's company.

. . . .

The winter came in early, with a great deal of cold and wet. There was snow, or sleet, or rain, almost every day for weeks, changing only for keen driving winds, or sharp frosts. The horses all felt it very much. Some of the drivers had a waterproof cover to throw over, which was a fine thing; but some of the men were so poor that they could not protect either themselves or their horses, and many of them suffered very much that winter. When we horses worked half the day we went to our dry stables, and could rest; whilst they had to sit on their boxes, sometimes staying out as late as one or two o'clock in the morning, if they had a party to wait for.

When the weather was very bad, many of the men would go and sit in the tavern close by, but they often lost a fare in that way, and could not, as Jerry said, be there without spending money. It was his opinion that spirits and beer made a man colder afterwards, and that dry clothes, good food, cheerfulness, and a comfortable wife at home, were the best things to keep a cabman warm. Polly always supplied him with something to eat when he could not get home, and sometimes he would see little Dolly peeping from the corner of the street, to make sure if "father" was on the stand. If she saw him, she would run off at full speed and soon come back with something in a tin or basket—some hot soup or pudding that Polly had ready. It was wonderful how such a little thing could get safely across the street, often thronged with horses and carriages; but she was a brave little maid, and felt it quite an honour to bring "father's first course," as he used to call it. She was a general favourite on the stand, and there was not a man who would not have seen her safely across the street, if Jerry had not been able to do it.

One cold, windy day, Dolly had brought
Jerry a basin of something hot, and was standing by him while he ate it. He had scarcely
begun when a gentleman, walking towards us
very fast, held up his umbrella. Jerry touched
his hat in return, gave the basin to Dolly, and
was taking off my cloth, when the gentleman,
hastening up, cried out, "No, no, finish your
soup, my friend; I have not much time to
spare, but I can wait till you have done, and
set your little girl safe on the pavement." So
saying, he seated himself in the cab. Jerry
thanked him kindly, and came back to Dolly.

"There, Dolly, that's a gentleman; that's a
real gentleman, Dolly; he has got time and
thought for the comfort of a poor cabman and
a little girl."

Jerry finished his soup, set the child across,
and then took his orders to drive. Several
times after that the same gentleman took our
cab. Sometimes he came round and patted
me, saying in his quiet, pleasant way, "This
horse has got a good master, and he deserves
it." It was a very rare thing for any one to
notice the horse that had been working for
him. I have known ladies to do it now and
then, and this gentleman, and one or two others have given me a pat and a kind word; but

ninety-nine out of a hundred would as soon think of patting the steam engine that drew the train.

.   .   .   .

One day, whilst our cab and many others were waiting outside one of the Parks, where a band was playing, a shabby old cab drove up beside ours. The horse was an old worn-out chestnut, with an ill-kept coat, and bones that showed plainly through it. The knees knuckled over, and the forelegs were very unsteady. I had been eating some hay, and the wind rolled a little lock of it that way, and the poor creature put out her long thin neck and picked it up, and then turned round and looked about for more. There was a hopeless look in the dull eye that I could not help noticing, and then, as I was thinking where I had seen that horse before, she looked full at me and said, "Black Beauty, is that you?"

It was Ginger! but how changed! The beautifully arched and glossy neck was now straight and lank, and fallen in, the clean straight legs and delicate fetlocks were swelled; the joints were grown out of shape with hard work; the face that was once so full of spirit and life, was now full of suffering, and I could tell by the heaving of her sides, and her frequent cough, how bad her breath was.

Our drivers were standing together a little way off, so I sidled up to her a step or two, that we might have a little quiet talk. It was a sad tale that she had to tell.

After a twelvemonth's run off at Earlshall, she was considered to be fit for work again, and was sold to a gentleman. For a little while she got on very well, but after a longer gallop than usual the old strain returned, and after being rested and doctored she was again sold. In this way she changed hands several times, but always getting lower down.

"And so at last," said she, "I was bought by a man who keeps a number of cabs and horses, and lets them out. You look well off, and I am glad of it, but I could not tell you what my life has been. When they found out my weakness, they said I was not worth what they gave for me, and that I must go into one of the low cabs, and just be used up; that is what they are doing, whipping and working with never one thought of what I suffer; they paid for me, and must get it out of me, they say. The man who hires me now pays a deal of money to the owner every day, and so he has to get it out of me too; and so it's all the week round and round, with never a Sunday rest."

I said, "You used to stand up for yourself if you were ill-used."

"Ah!" she said, "I did once, but it's no use; men are strongest, and if they are cruel and have no feeling, there is nothing that we can do, but just bear it, bear it on and on to the end. I wish the end was come, I wish I was dead. I have seen dead horses, and I am sure they do not suffer pain."

I was very much troubled, and I put my nose up to hers, but I could say nothing to comfort her. I think she was pleased to see me, for she said, "You are the only friend I ever had."

Just then her driver came up, and with a tug at her mouth backed her out of the line and drove off, leaving me very sad indeed.

A short time after this a cart with a dead horse in it passed our cab stand. The head hung out of the cart-tail, the lifeless tongue was slowly dropping with blood; and the sunken eyes! but I can't speak of them, the sight was too dreadful. It was a chestnut horse with a long thin neck. I saw a white streak down the forehead. I believe it was Ginger; I hoped it was, for then her troubles

would be over. Oh! if men were more merciful, they would shoot us before we came to
such misery.

.   .   .   .

Christmas and the New Year are very merry
times for some people; but for cabmen and
cabmen's horses it is no holiday, though it
may be a harvest. There are so many parties,
balls, and places of amusement open, that the
work is hard and often late. Sometimes driver
and horse have to wait for hours in the rain or
frost, shivering with cold, while the merry
people within are dancing away to the music.

On the evening of the New Year, we had to
take two gentlemen to a house in one of the
West End Squares. We set them down at nine
o'clock and were told to come again at eleven.
"But," said one of them, "you may have to
wait a few minutes, but don't be late."

As the clock struck eleven we were at the
door, for Jerry was always punctual. The
clock chimed the quarters—one, two, three,
and then struck twelve, but the door did not
open.

The wind had been very changeable, with
squalls of rain during the day, but now it came
on a sharp driving sleet. Still the clock chimed
the quarters, and no one came. At half-past

twelve, he rang the bell and asked the servant if he would be wanted that night.

"Oh! yes, you'll be wanted safe enough," said the man, "you must not go, it will soon be over."

At a quarter past one the door opened, and the two gentlemen came out; they got into the cab without a word, and told Jerry where to drive, that was nearly two miles. When the men got out they never said they were sorry to have kept us waiting so long, but were angry at the charge: they had to pay for the two hours and a quarter waiting; but it was hard-earned money to Jerry.

At last we got home; he could hardly speak, and his cough was dreadful; he could hardly get his breath, but he gave me a rub down as usual, and even went up into the hayloft for an extra bundle of straw for my bed.

It was late the next morning before anyone came, and then it was only Harry. At noon he came again, and gave us our food and water: this time Dolly came with him; she was crying, and I could gather from what they said that Jerry was dangerously ill, and the doctor said that he must never go back to the cab work again if he wished to be an old man.

It was quickly settled that as soon as Jerry was well enough, they should remove to the country, and that the cab and horses should be sold as soon as possible.

The day came for going away. Jerry had not been allowed to go out yet, and I never saw him after that New Year's Eve. Polly and the children came to bid me good-bye. "Poor old Jack! dear old Jack! I wish we could take you with us," she said, and then, laying her hand on my mane, she put her face close to my neck and kissed me. Dolly was crying and kissed me too. Harry stroked me a great deal, but said nothing, only he seemed very sad, and so I was led away to my new place.

Part Four

I WAS SOLD to a corn dealer and baker, whom Jerry knew, and with him he thought I should have good food and fair work. In the first he was quite right, and if my master had always been on the premises, I do not think I should have been overloaded, but there was a foreman who was always hurrying and driving every one, and frequently when I had quite a full load, he would order something else to be taken on. My carter's name was Jakes. Like the other carters, he always had the bearing rein up, which prevented me from drawing easily, and by the time I had been there three or four months, I found the work telling very much on my strength.

One day, I was loaded more than usual, and part of the road was a steep uphill: I used all my strength, but I could not get on, and was obliged continually to stop. This did not please my driver, and he was flogging me cruelly, when a lady stepped quickly up to him, and said: "Oh! pray do not whip your good horse any more; I am sure he is doing all he can, and the road is very steep. You see, you do not give him a fair chance; he cannot use all his power with his head held back as it is with that bearing rein; if you would take it off, I am sure he would do better—*do* try it."

"Well, well," said Jakes, with a short laugh, "anything to please a lady of course."

The rein was taken off, and in a moment I put my head down to my very knees. What a comfort it was! Then I tossed it up and down several times to get the aching stiffness out of my neck.

"Poor fellow! that is what you wanted," said she, patting and stroking me with her gentle hand. Jakes took the rein—"Come on, Blackie." I put down my head and threw my whole weight against the collar; I spared no strength; the load moved on, and I pulled it steadily up the hill, and then stopped to take breath.

The lady had walked along the footpath, and now came across into the road. She stroked and patted my neck, as I had not been patted for many a long day.

"You see he was quite willing when you gave him the chance; I thank you for trying my plan with your good horse, and I am sure you will find it far better than the whip. Good-day," and with another soft pat on my neck she stepped lightly across the path, and I saw her no more.

"That was a real lady, I'll be bound for it," said Jakes to himself; "she spoke just as polite as if I was a gentleman, and I'll try her plan, uphill, at any rate"; and I must do him the justice to say that he let my rein out several holes, and going uphill after that he always gave me my head; but the heavy loads went on. Good feed and fair rest will keep one's strength under full work, but no horse can stand against overloading; and I was getting so thoroughly pulled down from this cause, that a younger horse was bought in my place. However, I escaped without any permanent injury and was sold to a large cab owner.

. . . .

I shall never forget my new master; he had black eyes, his mouth was as full of teeth as a bulldog's, and his voice was as harsh as the grinding of cart wheels over gravel stones. His name was Nicholas Skinner.

Skinner had a low set of cabs and a low set of drivers; he was hard on the men, and the men were hard on the horses. In this place we had no Sunday rest, and it was in the heat of summer.

My life was now so utterly wretched that I wished I might, like Ginger, drop down dead at my work, and be out of my misery; and one day my wish very nearly came to pass.

I went on the stand at eight in the morning, and had done a good share of work, when we had to take a fare to the railway. A long train was just expected in, and as all the cabs were soon engaged, ours was called for. There was a party of four; a noisy, blustering man with a lady, a little boy, and a young girl, and a great deal of luggage. The lady and the boy got into the cab, and while the man ordered about the luggage, the young girl came and looked at me.

"Papa," she said, "I am sure this poor horse cannot take us and all our luggage so far, he is so very weak and worn out. Do look at him."

"Nonsense, Grace, get in at once, and don't make all this fuss; there, get in and hold your tongue!"

My gentle friend had to obey; and box after box was dragged up and lodged on the top of the cab, or settled by the side of the driver. At last all was ready, and with his usual jerk at the rein, and slash of the whip, he drove out of the station.

I got along fairly till we came to Ludgate Hill, but there the heavy load and my own

"I am sure this poor horse cannot take us
and all our luggage so far."

exhaustion were too much. I was struggling to keep on, when, in a single moment—I cannot tell how—my feet slipped from under me, and I fell heavily to the ground on my side; the suddenness and the force with which I fell seemed to beat all the breath out of my body. I heard a sort of confusion round me, loud, angry voices, and the getting down of the luggage, but it was all like a dream. I thought I heard that sweet, pitiful voice saying, "Oh! that poor horse! it is our fault." I cannot tell how long I lay there, but I found my life coming back, and a kind-voiced man was patting me and encouraging me to rise. After one or two attempts, I staggered to my feet, and was gently led to some stables which were close by.

In the evening I was sufficiently recovered to be led back to Skinner's stables. In the morning Skinner came with a farrier to look at me. He examined me very closely and said: "This is a case of overwork more than disease. If he was broken-winded, you had better have him killed out of hand, but he is not; there is a sale of horses coming off in about ten days. If you rest him and feed him up, you may get more than his skin is worth, at any rate."

Upon this advice, Skinner, rather unwillingly, I think, gave orders that I should be well fed and cared for, and when the twelfth day after the accident came, I was taken to the sale, a few miles out of London. I felt that any change from my present place must be an improvement, so I held up my head, and hoped for the best.

.   .   .   .

At this sale, of course I found myself in company with the old, broken-down horses— some lame, some broken-winded, some old, and some that I am sure it would have been merciful to shoot.

The buyers and sellers too, looked not much better off than the poor beasts they were bargaining about. Some of them looked as if poverty and hard times had hardened them all over; but there were others that I would have willingly used the last of my strength in serving; poor and shabby, but kind and human, with voices that I could trust. Coming from the better part of the fair, I noticed a man who looked like a gentleman farmer, with a young boy by his side. When he came up to me and my companions, he stood still, and gave a pitiful look round upon us. I saw his eye rest on me; I had still a good mane and tail, which did something for my appearance. I pricked my ears and looked at him.

"There's a horse, Willie, that has known better days." He put out his hand and gave me a kind pat on the neck. I put out my nose in answer to his kindness; the boy stroked my face.

"Poor old fellow! see, grandpapa, how well he understands kindness."

The man who had brought me for sale now put in his word. "This 'ere hoss is just pulled down with overwork in the cabs; he's not an old one, and I heerd as how the vetenary should say, that a six months' run off would set him right up. I've had the tending of him these ten days past, and a gratefuller, pleasanter animal I never met with, and 'twould be worth a gentleman's while to give a five-pound note for him, and let him have a chance. I'll be bound he'd be worth twenty pounds next spring."

The farmer slowly felt my legs, which were much swelled and strained; then he looked at my mouth. "Thirteen or fourteen, I should say; just trot him out, will you?"

I arched my poor thin neck, raised my tail a little, and threw out my legs as well as I could, for they were very stiff.

"'Tis a speculation," said the old gentleman,

shaking his head, but at the same time slowly drawing out his purse—"quite a speculation! Have you any more business here?" he said, counting the sovereigns into his hand.

"No, sir, I can take him for you to the inn, if you please."

"Do so, I am now going there."

They walked forward, and I was led behind. The boy could hardly control his delight, and the old gentleman seemed to enjoy his pleasure. I had a good feed at the inn, and was then gently ridden home by a servant of my new master's and turned into a large meadow with a shed in one corner of it.

Mr. Thoroughgood, for that was the name of my benefactor, gave orders that I should have hay and oats every night and morning, and the run of the meadow during the day, and "you, Willie," said he, "must take the oversight of him; I give him in charge to you."

The boy was proud of his charge, and undertook it in all seriousness. There was not a day when he did not pay me a visit. He always came with kind words and caresses, and of course I grew very fond of him. He called me Old Crony. Sometimes he brought his grandfather, who always looked closely at my legs: "This is our point, Willie," he would say; "but he is improving so steadily that I think we shall see a change for the better in the spring."

The perfect rest, the good food, the soft turf, and gentle exercise soon began to tell on my condition and my spirits. During the winter my legs improved so much that I began to feel quite young again. The spring came round, and one day in March Mr. Thoroughgood determined that he would try me in the phaeton. I was well pleased, and he and Willie drove me a few miles. My legs were not stiff now, and I did the work with perfect ease.

"He's growing young, Willie; we must give him a little gentle work now; he has a beautiful mouth, and good paces, they can't be better."

"Oh! grandpapa, how glad I am you bought him!"

"So am I, my boy, but he has to thank you more than me; we must now be looking out for a quiet, genteel place for him, where he will be valued."

·   ·   ·   ·   ·   ·   ·   ·   ·   ·   ·

One day during this summer the groom cleaned and dressed me with such extraordinary care that I thought some new change must be at hand. Willie seemed half anxious, half merry, as he got into the chaise with his grandfather.

"If the ladies take to him," said the old gentleman, "they'll be suited, and he'll be suited: we can but try."

At the distance of a mile or two from the village, we came to a pretty, low house, with a lawn and shrubbery at the front and a drive up to the door. Willie rang the bell, and asked if Miss Blomefield, or Miss Ellen was at home. Yes, they were. So, whilst Willie stayed with me, Mr. Thoroughgood went into the house. In about ten minutes he returned, followed by three ladies. They all came and looked at me and asked questions. The younger lady—that was Miss Ellen—took to me very much; she said she was sure she should like me, I had such a good face. It was then arranged that I should be sent for the next day.

In the morning a smart-looking young man came for me. I was led home, placed in a comfortable stable, fed and left to myself. The next day, when my groom was cleaning my face, he said: "That is just like the star that Black Beauty had, he is much the same height too; I wonder where he is now."

A little further on he came to the place in my neck where I was bled, and where a little knot was left in the skin. He almost started, and began to look me over carefully, talking to himself.

"White star in the forehead, one white foot on the off side, this little knot just in that place"—then looking at the middle of my back—"and as I am alive, there is that little patch of white hair that John used to call 'Beauty's three-penny bit.' It *must* be Black Beauty! Why, Beauty! Beauty! do you know me? little Joe Green that almost killed you?" And he began patting and patting me as if he was quite overjoyed.

I could not say that I remembered him, for now he was a fine-grown young fellow, with black whiskers and a man's voice, but I was sure he knew me, and that he was Joe Green, and I was very glad. I put my nose up to him, and tried to say that we were friends. I never saw a man so pleased.

"Give you a fair trial! I should think so indeed! I wonder who the rascal was that broke your knees, my old Beauty! You must have been badly served out somewhere; well, well, it won't be my fault if you haven't good times of it now. I wish John Manly was here to see you."

In the afternoon I was put into a low Park chair and brought to the door. Miss Ellen was going to try me, and Green went with her. I soon found that she was a good driver, and she seemed pleased with my paces. I heard Joe telling her about me, and that he was sure I was Squire Gordon's old Black Beauty.

When we returned, the other sisters came out to hear how I had behaved myself. She told them what she had just heard, and said: "I shall certainly write to Mrs. Gordon, and tell her that her favourite horse has come to us. How pleased she will be!"

After this I was driven every day for a week or so, and as I appeared to be quite safe Miss Lavinia at last ventured out in the small close carriage. After this it was quite decided to keep me and call me by my old name of "Black Beauty."

I have now lived in this happy place a whole year. Joe is the best and kindest of grooms. My work is easy and pleasant, and I feel my strength and spirits all coming back again. Mr. Thoroughgood said to Joe the other day: "In your place he will last till he is twenty years old—perhaps more."

Willie always speaks to me when he can, and treats me as his special friend. My ladies have promised that I shall never be sold, and so I have nothing to fear; and here my story ends. My troubles are all over, and I am at home; and often before I am quite awake, I fancy I am still in the orchard at Birtwick, standing with my old friends under the apple trees.